J.J. Jarves

Letters relating to a Collection of Pictures

SALZWASSER
VERLAG

J.J. Jarves

Letters relating to a Collection of Pictures

Reprint of the original, first published in 1859.

1st Edition 2022 | ISBN: 978-3-37513-286-6

Verlag (Publisher): Salzwasser Verlag GmbH, Zeilweg 44, 60439 Frankfurt, Deutschland
Vertretungsberechtigt (Authorized to represent): E. Roepke, Zeilweg 44, 60439 Frankfurt, Deutschland
Druck (Print): Books on Demand GmbH, In de Tarpen 42, 22848 Norderstedt, Deutschland

LETTERS

RELATING TO A

COLLECTION OF PICTURES

MADE BY

MR. J.-J. JARVES.

———•———

CAMBRIDGE:
PRIVATELY PRINTED.
1859.

INTRODUCTORY NOTE.

THE following papers, relating to the collection of pictures formed by Mr. Jarves, are printed in order to present to those interested to obtain such a gallery for Boston the information necessary as a basis for action.

In compliance with a request to that effect from Mr. Jarves, I would beg those to whom this pamphlet may be sent to consider that part of his letter which relates to the value set upon his pictures, and the terms of his offer, as a private communication. If the proposal made by Mr. Jarves should be accepted, there would be no further need of privacy.

It is greatly to be hoped that such an opportunity of obtaining for Boston a gallery of specimens of the best Italian Art may not be lost, and that Mr. Jarves's very generous proposition may be at once accepted.

CHARLES ELIOT NORTON.

Sept. 27, 1859.

CONTENTS.

LETTERS.

FLORENCE, August 26, 1859.

MY DEAR SIR:

IT has long been a pet scheme of mine to ini-
tiate in Boston a permanent gallery of paintings, with
particular reference to the chronology, motives, and
technical progress of Art, from the earliest development
in Italy of the Christian idea,/ until its climax in the
matured genius of its several illustrious schools. Master-
pieces it was hopeless to expect to secure. Researches,
however, made for my private studies, showed me that
it was feasible for one on the spot to get together a valuable collection of pictures, covering the ground from
the tenth to the sixteenth century, characteristic of the
great masters and their schools, illustrating the history of
Art, provided it were gone about promptly, quietly, and
diligently. Unwilling to lose the opportunity, I decided
on taking the responsibility upon myself of making such
a collection and of its subsequent adoption by my towns-
men. My own means being inadequate, I borrowed a
sufficient sum to warrant the undertaking, being per-

suaded, that, should my project fail as regarded Boston, the pictures would always be valuable in the European market. I lost no time in going systematically to work to secure genuine specimens of Byzantine and Græco-Italian paintings, and so in chiefly following the current of the Florentine, Sienese, and Umbrian schools to the time of Raffael. My adventures in this pursuit were often curious and instructive. They involved an inquisition into the intricacies of numberless villas, palaces, convents, churches, and household dens, all over this portion of Italy; the employment of many agents to scent out my prey; many fatiguing journeyings; miles upon miles of wearisome staircases; dusty explorations of dark retreats; dirt, disappointment, fraud, lies, and money often fruitlessly spent; all compensated, however, by the gradual accumulation of a valuable gallery. It sometimes happened that the search for some indispensable master in the series cost more time and money than would have secured many more popular names, though of less true merit. On one occasion, to get nine pictures, I was obliged to purchase a gallery of upwards of two hundred; the unnecessary ones being sold at auction in England. On another, having discovered a fine old Pollajuolo, the owner would not let me have it, unless I bought all in the room, (forty-four in number,) which also went to auction. I discovered a hoard of four thousand pictures got together a century ago by an eccentric Abbé who bought everything brought to him. They had been inherited by an aged miser, from whom, with painful negotiation, I obtained a fine altar-piece by Ridolfo Ghirlandajo and other pictures. In the lumber-room of a famous convent I chanced upon a beautiful Perugino, so smoked and dirtied as to be cast aside by the monks, who, for a consideration, gladly let me bear it away, and which, upon cleaning, proved to be untouched, and one of his finest compositions. It was a small easel picture. A beautiful full-length portrait of a Spanish grandee, by Velasquez, was found among the earth and rubbish of a noble villa, cut out from its frame, crusted with dirt, but beneath in fine preservation. But as I have written a chapter on the Acquisition and Authentication of Pictures in a History of the Italian Schools that I am preparing for the press, I will not prolong this part of my letter. Suffice it to say that the collection has become sufficiently interesting and valuable to attract the encomiums of distinguished amateurs from various countries and obtain proposals for advantageous sales. I will give a few details of the principal pictures.

A Byzantine Triptych, 12th century, containing Descent into Hades, Transfiguration and Wanderings of Israelites, etc., is for preservation and beauty a unique specimen, so far as my knowledge extends. It demonstrates a condition of Art greatly in advance of corresponding Italian, uniting the strength of Orgagna to the miniature delicacy of Fra Angelico.

An altar-piece, A. D. 1190, of Græco-Italian school, a mystic painting of rare beauty and singular excellence; engraved in Fumagalli's "*Museo di Pitture*," plate 1035, vol. 13, and fully described. A tripartite picture of the tenth century, very characteristic and rare, — nothing corresponding to it in collections here. Migliarini says, from the character of the cross on it (⍬), it may date back as far as the seventh century. Another curious Triptych anterior to Cimabue, containing nineteen compositions from Lives of Christ and St. John Baptist.

An altar-piece by Margaritone, (1240,) seven compositions, perfect, naïve, and curious. A beautiful specimen of Cimabue; Story of S. Nicolo di Bari. Annunciation, by Pietro Cavallini. Entombment, (altar-piece,) by Giotto. A magnificent Triptych, five feet high, painted for the noble Vecchietta family, with a document, ascribing it to Giotto, of the family from whom I purchased it; but the color is more like the Paduan *Giotteschi*, deep and rich, in fine preservation. Two fine specimens of Puccio Capanna; ditto of Taddeo and Agnolo Gaddi; ditto of Orgagna (for which an offer was made by Sir Charles Eastlake); ditto of Giottino, uncommonly fine, both in subjects and preservation, one of them from the Rinuccini Gallery. A small altar-piece, by Fra Angelico; a noble Duccio of Siena, a Diptych; Spinello Aretino, a Crucifixion; and numerous other pictures of importance, as illustrating some special Christian motive or local style.

Among the Sienese, a gem of an altar-piece by Simone di Martino (Memmi) an Epiphany, with *gradino;* the drawing of this is in the Uffizii. Of Sano di Pietro, the equal of Fra Angelico, two as fine specimens as Italy can show: the Coronation, thirty-six figures, and the Journey of the Magi.

Sassetto, Giovanni di Paolo, Matteo da Siena, Taddeo di Bartolo, a unique and magnificent Assumption of the Virgin, by Ambrogio Lorenzetti, a gem of mystic art, etc., represent the Purists. For the Naturalists, tracing the progress of landscape, mythological and historical painting, I have beautiful specimens by Paolo Uccello, Dello, Gozzoli, and a singular picture, a Bridal-Waiter, painted for the Piccolomini of Siena, by Pinturicchio ; The Disarming of Cupid, a signed picture, by Gentile da Fabriano ; Tabernacle picture by Masolino ; fragment of a *gradino* by Masaccio, figures wonderful for their vigorous naturalness ; a Botticelli, not excelled in beauty and perfection by any in Florence; Pollajuolo, Filippino, Fra Filippo, Lorenzo di Credi (an injured altar-piece, and a perfect easel-picture in his best manner); Piero di Cosimo, Andrea del Sarto (altar-piece and a fresco, the latter injured); Franciabigio, Pontormo, Beccafumi, Albertinelli, Granacci, Luca Signorelli ; a fresco of Domenico Ghirlandajo, perfect; Giovanni Bellini ; Squarcione; Giorgione, wonderful in color, — a Circumcision ; Cesare da Sesto, etc., etc.

To you, who are familiar with these artists, their names will convey an adequate idea of the scope of the collection. In condition, they are, as a whole, purer than those of the galleries, and, are favorable specimens of the masters they represent, outside of their greatest works.

Authentic documents seldom accompany pictures; fictitious, often. I have piles of documentary evidence, opinions, etc., but my chief reliance is internal proof. My own judgment, after many years' conscientious study in the presence of acknowledged originals, and constant association with experienced artists and amateurs, has with myself considerable weight. Besides, I fortify it by the opinions and testimony of the best European judges, — my sole desire being historic truth, unbiased by any preconceived theory or enthusiasm for one specialty of Art over another. Hence, in several cases, my pictures have names of less weight than might pass current with observers in general, or which, imitating the custom of public galleries, I might with impunity adopt. Thus, one of my most remarkable paintings is ascribed by good judges to Botticelli, or Pietro Pollajuolo, names of pecuniary weight in the picture-market; but my own studies lead me to ascribe it to Francesco di Martino of Siena, a name little known, though the picture in question is worthy of either of the other painters.

One of my most interesting is a *Pietà*, bought of the Chigi family as a Perugino, but which subsequent examination, confirmed by high opinions, leads me to ascribe to Raffael, before he was sixteen, from a design of his master's, with variations.

The Perugino already referred to is the Baptism of Christ, the Almighty and angels overhead.

Other pictures in the collection are an Ecce Homo by Sodoma, equal to anything of the kind by Raffael, — and one of his lovely Madonnas, the type being superior to his rival's; a noble picture by Paul Veronese, from the Pisani Gallery; a Crucifixion by Rubens, solemn in color, and remarkable for its horses and dogs; a large altar-piece of Fra Bartolommeo, painted for the Antinori family, rich in color, with broad landscape containing the histories of Christ subsequent to the Resurrection; and, lastly, a Leonardo, a Holy Family, referred to in one of his own letters, inherited by a will recorded at Florence by the gentleman from whom it came to me through the intervention of one party only.

I affix an estimate of value upon the pictures, based

upon my experience of the market, though less than I should demand, were the collection to be sold on speculation.

The Leonardo has been estimated by Baron Garriod at 100,000 francs, as the price I ought to receive for it, whenever fairly made known. Rio puts it at £2,000. I value it, at the lowest, say 10,000 dollars.

The Leonardo,	$10,000	Masolino,	$225
Fra Bartolommeo,	8,000	Masaccio,	450
Perugino,	2,000	Lorenzo di Credi,	750
Sodoma, Ecce Homo,	2,500	2 Organga,	600
" Holy Family,	1,000	Giotto, Triptych,	1,000
Velasquez,	2,000	Lorenzetti, Entombment,	400
Botticelli,	1,500	" Assumption,	600
Sano di Pietro, Coronation,	1,500	Lo Spagna,	600
" " Epiphany,	1,200	G. Bellini,	850
Paul Veronese,	500	Giorgione,	250
Fra Angelico,*	750	(?)	400
Byzantine Triptych,	125	2 Paolo Uccello,	600
Gentile da Fabriano,	600	Dello,	400
Ridolfo Ghirlandajo,	800	Giovanni di Paolo,	150
Domenico Ghirlandajo,	800	Sassetto,	100
Andrea del Sarto,	500	Simone Memmi	750
Raffael, youthful,	450	Margaritone,	200
Matteo da Siena,	400	Altar-Piece,	820
	34,125		8,145
			34,125

Remainder of Collection, say seventy-five others, at 9,000

In Boston, Murillo, 5,000 }
S. Rosa, 600 } 6,800
Sundry others, 700 }

57,570

Besides a number set aside for sale or exchange, being duplicates of masters, or not necessary, but which *cost* upwards of 2,000

$59,570

In round numbers, I value the entire collection at $60,000, which is much less than it would be held at in the hands of dealers, and considerably under the rates at

* The companion piece is held at 1,320 dollars by the owner.

which Messrs. Lombardi & Ugobaldi sold their early masters to the National Gallery, viz.: $36,000 for twenty pictures. I am now urged to put prices upon the pictures by an agent from London recommended by Sir Charles Eastlake. I still cling to my original project; but if my fellow-citizens do not consider in a favorable light the proposition I authorize you to make in my behalf, I shall soon be compelled to consent to the sale of at least a portion of the gallery in England or Russia, because, as one always does in such affairs, I exceeded my original limits, and the interest money I must pay is heavier than I can continue long to afford. It would gratify me, however, to have my estimate amended or confirmed by judicious judges. Perhaps the fairest method would be to select three, — an amateur, artist, and dealer; the several kinds of valuation would then be represented, and an average could be struck. I am persuaded that for $60,000 it would be impossible now to get together a collection of equal value. Indeed, some of the pictures parted with, it would be out of the question to hope to replace them. I have worked hard for several years, with extraordinary facilities for their collection, — my entire time, energies, and all the money I could control being devoted to it; and nothing less than the enthusiasm I feel for Art, and the desire to aid in forming an institution worthy of the intellectual claims of Boston, *unique* of its kind in America, has sustained me thus far. You fully comprehend that this sort of labor can neither be incited nor repaid by pecuniary gain; and though I might finally realize a handsome profit from its sale, still it would be at the cost of much feeling. To obviate this and secure my aim, I propose, for $20,000, to deliver the collection, with a descriptive catalogue, published in connection with my History of the Schools of Painting represented by the Gallery, (copyrights of both to be mine, with the privilege of illustration from the pictures,) in good order, either in Italy or Boston, (if the latter, actual expenses to be paid, of packing, freight, and insurance,) to any association or individuals pledged to make it finally the nucleus of a permanent gallery for Boston, the final arrangement for exhibition (hanging, lights, and temperature, — the last an important consideration for pictures on wood) to be intrusted to me, and the collection to be kept together as a whole, under some distinctive name. Or, including the above conditions, a committee, as above suggested, being appointed to appraise the pictures, I will give one half of their appraisal for the above purpose, the other half being paid to me.

Further, as it is desirable to increase the value and efficiency of the gallery by the addition of masters of the Venetian, Lombard, and Bolognese schools, illustrating the gradual decline of Art in Italy, if funds be raised for that end, I agree to give my time and experience (travelling-expenses paid) to their acquisition. I have on my list several valuable paintings, known only to a few, which the exhaustion of my means alone has prevented me from obtaining. Among them a fine Giorgione, Titian, and an undoubted Raffael, — second manner, somewhat injured, but untouched. The subject, Vision of St. Bernard, the Madonna introduced being that of the Foligno. It was the *gradino* of one of his altar-pieces. But these or others must be approached with much caution, as Italian imaginations are never more vivid than in regard to the prices of works of Art, especially if sought for by strangers.

For a sum not exceeding $50,000, I can secure for Boston, including my own, a highly respectable gallery of Italian Art, consisting of from one hundred and fifty to two hundred genuine paintings, embracing many good specimens of the best masters, provided the means be *promptly* and *quietly* furnished. Mr. E. N. Perkins tells me that the common Athenæum exhibitions have netted from $2,000 to $3,000 yearly to that institution. Would not the exhibition of such a gallery as I propose, supposing it was considered advisable to put on it a small admittance fee for the present, produce a handsome fund for ulterior purposes? — and would it not greatly benefit Boston by attracting visitors from all parts of the Union? While some public-spirited citizens of New York have been debating the buying of the Campana Gallery of Rome, the Russian government has taken it at $1,340,000. Boston pays $10,000 for a statue, and $8,000 for a picture of Copley's. Surely, then, it is not too much to hope that her large-minded men should be willing to contribute $50,000 to inaugurate a Public Gallery, beginning with some two hundred paintings, embracing a history of the Italian schools for five centuries; or, if that be too large an idea for the present, $20,000 for those that I possess; which price even would make me an actual contributor of *nearly one-third their entire cost.* My sole motive in mentioning this is to show that I am in earnest, and to stimulate others.

It was my intention to return to Boston the coming autumn, but I shall probably be detained here another year. My time here may be usefully devoted to the enlargement of the gallery, as has been suggested. The locality and history of every picture this way to be procured are well known to me.

Faithfully yours,

JAMES J. JARVES.

CHARLES E. NORTON, Esq.

LETTER OF MR. C. C. BLACK.

July, 1859.

MY DEAR NORTON:

WHEN Goldsmith laid down, as one of the two rules by which a reputation for connoisseurship might be attained, that the aspirant must praise the works of Pietro Perugino, we may presume he did so, not from any accurate appreciation he himself possessed of that old painter's merits, but rather that he selected the name as that of a recondite and rarely investigated luminary in the galaxy of Art. Keener eyes and better æsthetic telescopes have, however, of late years, been directed towards the pictorial sky, and Perugino's name would now stand far down, were we to catalogue the lights which shine from distances beyond the orbits even of Giotto and Cimabue, till the gazer is finally bewildered among Sienese nebulæ and Byzantine star-dust. These thoughts came on me forcibly, on crossing the Piazza Maria Antonia, after a by no means thorough examination of the very interesting collection formed by our friend J. J. Jarves. Although I think you visited it, when in Florence some years ago, his untiring energy has added to it so largely since you were among us, that I am minded to give you (without much pretence to chronological accuracy) some notes of a few chief objects of my admiration.

Though aware that Mr. Jarves had confined his purchases principally to the more ancient masters, proposing —and wisely—to illustrate the germ and growth of Modern Art, I was not prepared for the distance to which skill and patience have carried him back, and found him, to my surprise, the possessor of one of the earliest known representations of the Crucifixion, dating from the tenth, or possibly the ninth century. By the way, in writing to one who is acquainted with the galleries of the Catacombs, I may enter a *caveat* against the accusation of inaccuracy, by explaining that I mean one of the earliest *movable* representations, excluding, of course, wall-paintings. Specimens of this date are naturally very rare ; some, however, there are, and well authenticated, one in particular in the Museum of Fine Arts at Florence, closely resembling this of Mr. Jarves. A marked and distinctive peculiarity is the form of the cross, which, indeed, can be termed so merely for convenience, as it is Y-shaped, curiously resembling the embroidery on a priestly stole, and figuring, moreover, in the shield of the Archbishop of Canterbury. To step from this strange relic of early piety to Margaritone of Arezzo may not be strictly chronological; but, as I said before, this I do not profess to be. This old master is represented here by a Virgin, attended by the Saints

Peter and Paul, the central painting surrounded with smaller ones, which show various events of their lives. Their martyrdoms in particular are packed with an economy of space truly wonderful. In singular contrast to the hard, rugged, Ben-Jonsonish energy of Margaritone is a Greek painting of very early date, (well known to collectors, and engraved by Fumagalli,) highly finished in detail, the jewels of the tiara and the folds of embroidered drapery quite wonderful, but the features smooth, polished, and insignificant as one of Hayley's poems. I was much pleased with a small Giovanni di Paolo, representing a female saint in gray who kneels to a Pope. How these old artists caught the keynote of character in their figures! It seems as though there was in the childhood of Art something analogous to the actual childhood of human life; for even as an observant child unfailingly selects the chief characteristic, bodily or mental, of a visitor, so do we find these early painters insisting on distinctive character as determinately as though they had just been reading the "Ars Poetica." We have here a demure train-bearer and a sulky cardinal, both of whom I have seen in Roman processions, Corpus Domini, for instance, times without number.

Duccio, whose noble picture at Siena hangs on the Cathedral walls so awkwardly as to be hardly visible, may be admired here much more satisfactorily, in a beautiful Virgin and Child, as also in a Crucifixion, showing what, to me, was a somewhat novel treatment of this much-worn subject. The chief personage among the spectators is a Roman soldier in all the gorgeous panoply of war, *sagum, paludamentum*, etc., etc., whose attitude of determination somewhat puzzled me till I bethought me of the centurion (called by the Church of Rome "Longinus") who declared, "Truly, this man was the Son of God!" If any doubt could exist, it would be removed by noticing the countenance of the soldier behind him. Wonder, horror, and the reserve generated by discipline, are all combined in his attitude ; and we may clearly see his consciousness that what in his captain may be but an unguarded word would in him be flat blasphemy. Perhaps no better example could be found, to show the soul these early masters put into their works, than the various expressions, gestures, and costumes here displayed on a space not larger than a sheet of letter-paper.

A Virgin and Child with a Goldfinch, which hangs near the Duccio, shows how much the Italian painters followed each other, or were, possibly, all led by some now obsolete tradition, in the accompaniments to their chief figures. This work is ascribed, doubtfully, to Giotto, who, however, contributes one indubitable Entombment. There is a Cimabue, genuine in style, and genuine in subject, too, as representing one of those delightful facts which occurred only in the "good old times,"—St. Nicholas throwing gold balls into the windows of poor, portionless maidens. You have Santa Claus still among you, and can tell whether he yet indulges in that beneficent play : I fear that the acquaintance our English poor have with gilded balls is of a less pleasing character.

Fra Angelico appears here unmistakably in a painting of three saints, St. Zenobio, St. Francis, and St. Thomas (I forget which of them) ; and an Adoration of the Magi, by Simone Memmi, would attract any one's notice, if only from a wonderful group of men, horses, and camels, thrust together in much-admired disorder. Some such group may have been seen by Shakspeare, in his mind's eye or otherwise, when he wrote the description of the tapestry in the "Rape of Lucrece," where "for Achilles' image stood a spear grasped in an armed hand."

I have really no time to expatiate on the various excellent specimens of painters, good and rare, such as Pietro Cavallini, Andrea Castagno, Matteo da Siena,—of whom we have a Virgin and Child, and happily not his oft-repeated and horribly elaborated Murder of the Innocents, —Taddeo Gaddi, who shows us St. Dominic receiving at the hands of St. Peter the sword he used so ruthlessly against heretics. Nor can I do more than offer to more leisurely speculation two quaint Byzantine tablets, in which Julian the Apostate is being speared by Mercourios (?), while Maxentius undergoes the same fate at the hand, not of Constantine, but of one Dicaterina, — St. Catharine, I suppose ; but let it pass. I must, however, do homage to Sano di Pietro, an artist whose works, even in Italy, must be sought with care, as nearly all the best are confined to his native city of Siena. Nevertheless we find here no less than three specimens of his handiwork,— an Adoration of Magi, a St. Margaret, wonderful in drapery, and a Coronation of the Virgin, so pure and sacred in feeling as to show at once his right to the title of the Sienese Fra Angelico. Of Filippo Lippi there is an Annunciation, in a state of preservation very uncommon,— and the same subject by Credi, clean and fresh in coloring as all his works are, and treated in a very pleasing, unconventional manner.

"*Omnia ex ovo*," says the old physiological adage; and I presume that the Virgin Mary herself forms no exception to the rule, unless, indeed, the dogma of the Immaculate Conception interfere,—a question which I beg to refer to his Holiness Pio Nono. At all events, here we have the Virgin, very pleasingly painted by a scholar of Albertinelli, inclosed in an egg,—not a *vesica piscis* glory, nor an oval mass of clouds, but a veritably well-painted egg,— the shell broken open at the side, the fractured edges carefully drawn, so as to display the figure. Leaving unsolved the mystic meaning of this very pretty picture, I pass to another Virgin and Child, delicate in coloring, and charming in expression, by Sandro Botticelli,—and to a small panel, liable to be overlooked by a casual observer, but very interesting as being not improbably the identical Birth of St. John painted by Masaccio and described in Vasari. The circumstantial evidence, with which I shall not trouble you, is very strong in its favor.

You know the man of many names: Sodoma to the world, Razzi of Siena to his familiars; and now, by favor of some of those confounded investigators who upset our faith in Romulus, Richard, Joan of Arc,—nay, even would do so in respect to Shakspeare himself,— Bazzi of Piedmont would seem to be the genuine name of the painter. Happily, these *rixæ de lanâ caprinâ* are very unimportant; the names may perish, but Romeo, Lear, Hamlet, and, though in an humbler sphere, the Chapel of San Bernardino at Siena, and the upper floor of the Farnesina at Rome, are undeniable facts. Mr. Jarves possesses a glorious Razzi, Christ bearing the Cross, almost as rich in coloring as the grand

fresco in the Belle Arti at Siena, and decidedly no-
bler in expression, — the point in which Sodoma was
most commonly weak. A proof of this assertion may
be seen by comparing his celebrated St. Catharine Faint-
ing, in the Dominican Church at Siena, with the same
subject as treated by Beccafumi in this gallery. Although
in many points closely resembling, and generally to the
advantage of Sodoma, the countenance of the Father in
Beccafumi's work is far grander. ·

Do you remember the shops of the *pizzicaroli* at
Rome during Passion Week, — those mysterious cav-
erns propped by sides of bacon, panelled with hams, and
roofed with numerous starry lamps twinkling from a
heaven of lard? If not, read Hans Anderssen's Impro-
visatore, or look with me at a picture of Masolino da
Panicale, where the Virgin is adoring her new-born infant in front of just such a cave. Though meant for
stone, the brown walls and whitish roof bear unmistak-
able traces of their adipose porcine models. Germany,
ever anxious to get a foothold in Italy, here sends, as her
representative, a Crucifixion, by F. Franck, — how oddly
the name resembles Francesco Francia! — richly colored,
carefully executed, and showing a wonderfully elaborate
background, where Jerusalem appears crowded with steep
roofs, golden weather-cocks, and pepper-box turrets.
Truly, the early Germans were no more solicitous as to
anachronisms than the later Italians; as witness a Crucifixion here by Paolo Veronese, and a Tintoretto, where
St. Agnes is unveiled by a knightly personage in rich
black armor of the fifteenth century. The painter has
somewhat softened the painful character of this subject

by the compassionate air which he has given to the warrior.

But I find my letter has already run to an unconscionable length. I have left myself no room to speak at all, as it deserves, of what is, perhaps, the most valuable gem of the whole gallery, an undoubted Leonardo da Vinci. You, who know that Leonardos are so rare that they may in general terms be declared quite unattainable,—albeit they figure in every catalogue as surely as Johannisberger in a Rhine-steamer's wine-list,—will be glad to learn that Migliarini, whose judgment cannot be called in question, adds the weight of his authority to the preponderating historical evidence of the authenticity of this work.

I should like to detail to you some of the gorgeous court-costumes devised by Paolo Uccello, to grace the pageant where King Solomon in all his glory meets the Queen of Sheba,—to speculate on the interpretation of a most perplexing and enticing allegory by Gentile da Fabriano, called the Triumph of Love, — and to speak more fully than is now possible of a beautiful female head by Cesare da Sesto, of a soldierly Velasquez, of a large and important Ridolfo Ghirlandajo.

Before concluding this very imperfect review, in which I have left quite unmentioned many interesting pictures, let me revert to our old friend Perugino, with whose name I began my letter, and of whom Mr. Jarves possesses a small but unmistakably genuine painting,—as also to our dearer friend Noll Goldsmith, whose other recipe was, " to observe that the picture would have been better, if the painter had taken more pains." How very safely this remark may yet be applied to the Caracci and their school ! Rarely, if ever, do we meet a work of the Bolognese school which does not, in spite of its unquestionable merit, offend by a certain careless air, which seems to show that the painter felt himself fully equal, nay, possibly superior, to the requirements of his subject. On the other hand, the conscientious labor, the solemn purity, visible in every portion of a painting by Duccio, Fra Angelico, or Sano di Pietro, impresses on us the conviction that these men felt called on to make a holocaust of the talent God had given them, in serving as best they could the Giver.

I must now conclude, and only hope that this imperfect summary may suffice to show what can be done, even at this late period of picture-hunting, when good judgment and activity are backed by patience and well-timed liberality.   C. C. BLACK.

LETTER OF MR. T. A. TROLLOPE, FROM THE LONDON ATHENÆUM OF 12TH FEBRUARY, 1859.

FLORENCE, January 20.

*   *   *   *   *

I WAS invited the other day to visit a gallery of pictures, the collection and object of which interested me much, and seemed strangely to indicate the apparently inexhaustible artistic wealth which has been stored up in these old Tuscan cities, as in a garner for the perennial supply of the entire world. They have furnished forth galleries for the delight and Art-instruction of every na-

tion of Europe. And now they are called on to perform
a similar civilizing office for the rising world on the other
side of the Atlantic. And to how great ·an extent they
are still able to answer to the demand, the collection I
am speaking of most surprisingly proves. It has been
brought together by an American gentleman, a Bostonian,
of the name of Jarves, and is destined to form the
nucleus of a public gallery in his native city, the young
Athens of America. The funds necessary for its collection have been furnished, I understand, by a public-spirited
lover of Art in Boston, with the view of supplying his
countrymen, before it is too late, with the means of obtaining a tolerably competent Art-education without the
necessity of crossing the Atlantic for it. One would
have thought that it had been already too late to accom-
plish so patriotic a purpose, were not the gallery in question here to prove the contrary. Sir Charles Eastlake,
I am told, when recently here, wistfully sounded the
owner as to the possibility of tempting him to relinquish
one or two of his treasures. But "the almighty dollar"
has already ceased, it seems, to be almighty in Boston;
for the answer was, that the collection would go unmu-
tilated to America.

This first attempt to make the New World a sharer in
the great Art-heritage of Europe's old civilization is a cir-
cumstance so interesting, and, in view of the special bent the
specimens obtained may give to an entire new lineage of
Art and artists, is so important, that it seems worth while
to say a few words of the nature and merit of the collection.

Mr. Jarves has been for some years a resident in Florence, and has devoted himself entirely to this object. In the pursuit of it, Yankee energy and industry were, as a matter of course, not wanting. But the very creditable knowledge and judgment manifested in expending the funds devoted to the object might, perhaps, have been less to be anticipated. And Boston has been very fortunate in being catered for by one of her citizens, perhaps the only one living who has given many years of his life to the study of Italian Art. But, most of all, the amazing good-fortune which has helped him in his aim will strike those who can appreciate the difficulty of obtaining specimens of many of the masters, who will be well represented in the Boston gallery.

Mr. Jarves has done wisely in seeking to make his collection especially illustrative of the history, progress, and, so to speak, genealogy of the Art; being aware that it is by such a study of its masters that an artist, as distinguished from an imitator, must be formed. He has also done well in paying particular attention to the condition of his specimens, preferring to have them with the mark of time upon them, when not such as to deface the master's sense and treatment, rather than to have more showy pictures at the cost of restoration amounting to re-painting.

The collection is especially rich in specimens, one or two of them almost, if not quite, unique, of the earliest days of revived Art. Some very curious Byzantine works of the tenth and subsequent centuries bring the history down to Margaritone da Arezzo, in 1240, who is represented by a most remarkable altar-piece. There is also a very important picture, as an historical document,

4

of date between 1198 and 1216, which may be found engraved in the 13th volume of Fumagalli's "Collection of the Principal Pictures of Europe."

Cimabue, Giotto, Duccio, Taddeo and Agnolo. Gaddi, Andrea Orgagna (a picture by him which Sir Charles Eastlake had previously sought to purchase), Gentile da Fabriano (a signed picture by this very rare artist, of whom not above eight works are known to be extant in Europe), Fra Angelico, Sano di Pietro, Masaccio (a fragment of a *predella* cited by Vasari), Fra Filippo Lippi, Botticelli, P. di Perugino, Lorenzo di Credi, Fra Bartolommeo (a very grand altar-piece), Leonardo da Vinci (Holy Family, with same character of background and about the same date as Lord Suffolk's *Vierge aux Rochers*, a very valuable and undoubtedly authentic work), Lo Spagna, Sodoma (two fine specimens), Pinturicchio, Domenico and Ridolfo Ghirlandajo, Raphael (a very interesting early work, painted by him while still with his master, Perugino, from a design of his, but with variations),— all these, and several other less generally known names, are represented. There are also some interesting portraits, especially a contemporary one of Fernando Cortés, and a full-length Spanish grandee in armor, by Velasquez.

It will be admitted that no ordinary degree of goodfortune must have been added to activity and judgment, to render feasible the collection of such an assemblage of genuine pictures at this time of day. Those who have attempted, with more or less success, to purchase pictures recently in Italy, will probably be not a little surprised that it should have been possible. And it may be safely asserted, that, if any other of the more wealthy communities of the United States, stimulated by the example and success of my Bostonian friend, should think, like Jack the Giant-killer's Cornish foe, "her can do that herself," and should attempt the feat with twice the pecuniary means, they will find that it is not to be repeated. And it is probable that the old Puritan city of New England will hereafter be the only community in America possessing a fair sample of ancient religious Art, — unless, indeed, some transatlantic Napoleon should, in the fulness of time, administer a course of "*idées Napoléoniennes*" to the cities of the Old World after the manner of the great original.

A very large quantity of painted canvas and wood has of late years been exported hence to the United States, to the great encouragement of our staple manufacture. But while the fact shows that the "demon," who "whispers, 'Have a taste,'" has crossed the Atlantic, the acquisitions hitherto made by the Great Republic have only proved the urgent need that some means of instruction, such as that here provided for Boston, should be furnished to the American Art-patrons who travel, as well as to the American artists who stay at home.

T. A. TROLLOPE.

ARTICLE FROM THE BOSTON COURIER OF 9TH FEBRUARY, 1859.

IT will be remembered that a few weeks ago there appeared in our columns a letter from a correspondent in Florence, speaking in very high terms of a collection of pictures, especially of the works of the early Italian artists, made by our townsman, Mr. James Jackson Jarves. Mr. Jarves has been for some years engaged in gathering together his acquisition, and his intention is to continue in the same pursuit for some years longer ; not with a view of accumulating a valuable collection which shall be held for the exclusive gratification of himself and his friends, and transmitted to his heirs, but with higher aims and ends. He wishes to employ it in such a way as to promote a taste for Art, and the cultivation of Art, among his countrymen ; and having been born and reared in Boston, he naturally prefers that his collection should have a resting-place here. His desire is, that it should be purchased by subscription, and form the nucleus and beginning of a free gallery of Art, for the benefit of the public and the instruction of artists. The possession of such a gallery, in combination with our public library, and the splendid museum of natural history which is destined to be reared at once in our immediate neighborhood, would give to Boston peculiar advantages for · bestowing upon its citizens that finished education which includes science, literature, and the fine arts, and make it proportionally attractive to strangers. In a community like ours, where wealth and political distinction are so eagerly pursued, — neither object of pursuit being very elevating or refining in its effects, — a public gallery of works of Art would shed a benignant and beneficent influence over all that came within its sphere, and thus tend to correct the hardening and narrowing tendencies which so much beset us.

With this view we have much pleasure in bringing this collection again to the notice of our readers, and in laying before them some testimony which proves, beyond question or cavil, its merit and importance. The first piece that we offer is a letter addressed to Mr. Jarves by Sir Charles Eastlake, President of the Royal Academy, a gentleman cautious alike by temperament and official position, and whose words may be fairly taken, therefore, to mean a little more than they say : —

7 FITZROY SQUARE, LONDON, 16th Nov., 1858.

DEAR SIR : —

I rejoice to hear that you propose to send your collection of specimens of early Italian masters, in its entire state, to America. Few would have taken the trouble you have gone through in discovering and obtaining these works. Your continued residence in Tuscany has enabled you to avail yourself of many excellent opportunities. Good-fortune has also sometimes rewarded you ; but to your discrimination and knowledge your success is chiefly to be ascribed.

I consider that the series in question would form an excellent foundation for a gallery of Italian Art, and I trust that in your native country it will be appreciated and kept together. I purposely avoid particularizing any works, because I have at all times uniformly declined to give any kind of certificate as regards single pictures; but I can conscientiously congratulate you on the formation of the collection as a whole. I believe that many valuable additions have been made to it even since I saw it.

Wishing you all success in your patriotic object, I am, dear Sir,

Your faithful servant,

C. L. EASTLAKE.

JAMES J. JARVES, Esq.

We next present a translation of a communication addressed to Mr. Jarves by Prof. Migliarini, director of the Uffizii Gallery, an artist of merit, and probably the very highest authority on Art in Italy. His observations are mostly confined to a single picture in Mr. Jarves's collection, which he affirms to be an original Leonardo da Vinci; and if so, we need not say that it is a possession of great rarity and great value. The technical and scientific character of Prof. Migliarini's remarks, though it may make them less interesting to the general reader, will, we trust, commend them all the more to our artist friends : —

FLORENCE, GALLERY OF THE UFFIZII, Oct. 15, 1858.

MY DEAR MR. JARVES : —

I hope you will allow me to express my satisfaction at the pleasure afforded me of admiring, on two different occasions, your rich collection of ancient paintings, in the acquisition of which, it appears to me, that a great deal has been owing to good-fortune; for, without this, perseverance and money would have been of little avail.

I will not enumerate the many different artists of whom you have obtained beautiful specimens, such as Cimabue, the Giotteschi, followed by Dello, il Pollajuolo, il Ghirlandajo, and many others; but among so many, I will confine myself to that gem of Leonardo da Vinci, which it seems to me incredible that you should have been able to fall in with and possess.

Every one knows that Da Vinci lived long, but, unfortunately, did little in painting; his attention having been distracted by the fortuitous circumstances in life, and more by the many other sciences he professed, in which he was also distinguished as a great genius. There are, thus, many galleries which boast of possessing some of his productions; but to the experienced eye of the connoisseur it very often happens, that, in view of the object decorated with so great a name, preconceived expectation of enjoyment is followed by the silent apathy of indifference, — and this, all the more, because he had disciples of great merit, who imitated him with much ability.

One of the striking peculiarities of your picture is, that it is unfinished, and in this condition it best proves its true originality. For, if one of Leonardo's best imitators had copied it, — while there could be no doubt in regard to the design, well known to be that of Leonardo, and his drawing of the Infant Saviour, " il Bambino," is well known, — he would have carried it to completion, either for pecuniary benefit, or gain in reputation.

But here I may be asked, if a copyist in such a case could not have left his copy unfinished. I am willing to admit this; but would ask my inquirer to reflect that whoever undertakes Leonardo's very difficult method of laying on the body colors would not dare to imitate those occasional dashes of the pencil, of which there appear clear indications in your picture, seeming to be mere memoranda for changes to be afterwards made at pleasure. He who copies so great an artist has always before his eyes the almost impossibility of imitating him, and consequently lacks the courage to paint with entire freedom.

Moreover, let it pass as a general rule, that all the imitators of Leonardo are apt to be low-toned; yet the lowest tone is never black; in its gradation towards the light it always inclines to the hue of bistre or tobacco color. This peculiar characteristic, it seems to me, had its origin in the experience which the most able masters of that time had in the bad effects of lamp-black, employed by Leonardo, and afterwards by Giulio Romano. These substituted other blacks, which, mixed with other colors, produce a shade tint.* On examination, your picture has no such appearance, but is really coal-black in the deep shadows, as is always the case with the works known to be of Da Vinci.

I shall probably be reminded of another style of Leonardo's, namely, that of his portraits, in which this

---

* The mixture of black, in the shadows, was soon found by experience to be a very pernicious practice, because the black gradually comes to the surface, obscuring the other colors with which it was mixed; and subsequent artists made it a rule to exclude black entirely from their shadows. Instead of black, they used a mixture of deep transparent colors, — blue, red, and yellow, mixed to a neutral tint.

intense blackness is seldom found. And this is quite natural, because he treated historical subjects in a different manner from portrait-painting. In his "Treatise on Painting," he often advises the sitter to be placed in a broad light, so that the features may not be cut up by too violent shadows. Is it possible that he would recommend to others what he did not practise himself? Hence it follows, that, in a broad light, he could dispense with the pernicious use of black, and, for this reason, many of his portraits are lighter and better preserved.

It is needless for me to enlarge on the beauties of this painting, as this would lead me into long digressions; and I should not wish to describe qualities of which it is impossible to give an approximate idea with the pen. I will only remark that the landscape is composed of many minute features, finished with great minuteness, in order that the figures of the Virgin and the Child may, by contrast, gain in grandeur of effect.

I will not mention Leonardo's peculiar grace and sweetness of expression, which has been frequently dilated upon by eminent writers. I will say nothing of the wonderful relief of his *chiaro oscuro*, of which language cannot give the slightest idea.

I therefore conclude, congratulating you on so beautiful and precious an acquisition; and begging you to receive kindly this expression of my admiration, I am, with many thanks for your civility,

Yours, etc.,

M. A. MIGLIARINI.

After reading the above, we think no one can doubt that Mr. Jarves has gathered together a valuable and interesting collection, such as every public-spirited citizen of Boston would be glad to see among us.

LETTER OF MONSIEUR A. F. RIO TO MR. JARVES.

MY DEAR SIR:

I HAVE not the least hesitation in declaring that I fully believe it the [Leonardo] to be the work of that great master. I cannot help envying your good-luck in making such a valuable acquisition. You could not begin your collection under better auspices. The genuine pictures of Leonardo are so rare, that the want of one has left to this day a sore gap in the gallery of many a sovereign.

You are quite right in trying to get pictures of the Sienese school, which has been, till now, less studied than the others, and which is growing more and more into repute. Your two pictures of Antonio Razzi (Sodoma) are quite sufficient to give an idea of that great painter, who has so often been compared with Raphael himself; but my weakness for the old school impels me to say that for my own gratification I should prefer your pictures of Sano di Pietro. A time will come when that charming master will be appreciated to his full value, and his works sought after as so many precious gems of mystical thought. France, England, and Germany know him only by reputation. I do not remember seeing a single picture of his in any of those countries. The specimen which you possess has two great advantages: it represents the painter's favorite subject, the Coronation of the Virgin, and is in perfect state of preservation. I have observed in your collection a charming little picture by Matteo di Giovanni. Your Gentile da Fabriano is, on account of its date, an important document in the history of that school; and I should place still higher the Madonna between four Saints, by Lo Spagna, who was the best pupil of Perugino, next to Raphael.

You will render the science of Art more accessible to those [in America] who cannot cross the seas to study it in its birth-place.

With the best wishes for the success of your patriotic undertaking,

Most sincerely yours,

Rio.*

---

* M. Rio is the well-known French writer, the author of an important work on Christian Art. His opinion justly carries great weight.